Rowan Barnes-Murphy's

MOTHER GOOSE

Rowan Barnes-Murphy's
MOTHER GOOSE

HODDER AND STOUGHTON
LONDON SYDNEY AUCKLAND TORONTO

Conceived, designed and produced by Signpost Books Ltd.
44 Uxbridge Street, London W8 7TG

Copyright in this format © 1989 Signpost Books Ltd.
Illustrations copyright © 1989 Rowan Barnes-Murphy
Designed by Rowan Barnes-Murphy

British Library Cataloguing in Publication Data

Rowan Barnes-Murphy's Mother goose.
1. Nursery rhymes in English
I. Barnes-Murphy, Rowan
398'.8

ISBN 0-340-50122-7

First published 1989

Published by Hodder and Stoughton Children's Books,
a division of Hodder and Stoughton Ltd,
Mill Road, Dunton Green, Sevenoaks, Kent TN13 2YA

Typeset by AKM Associates (UK) Ltd
Ajmal House, Hayes Road, Southall

To Frankie

AT BRILL ON THE HILL

At Brill on the hill
The wind blows shrill,
The cook no meat can dress;
At Stow-on-the-Wold
The wind blows cold,
I know no more than this.

BAT, BAT, COME UNDER MY HAT

Bat, bat, come under my hat,
And I'll give you a slice of bacon;
And when I bake, I'll give you a cake,
If I am not mistaken.

THE APPLE TREE

As I went up the apple tree
All the apples fell on me;
Bake a pudding, bake a pie,
Send it up to John MacKay;
John MacKay is not in,
Send it up to the man in the moon.

Baa, Baa, Black Sheep

Baa, baa, black sheep,
Have you any wool?
Yes, sir, yes, sir,
Three bags full;

One for the master,
And one for the dame,
And one for the little boy
Who lives down the lane.

The Cock's On The Wood Pile

The cock's on the wood pile a-blowing his horn,
The bull's in the barn a-threshing of corn,
The maids in the meadows are making of hay,
The ducks in the river are swimming away.

11

MOTHER, MAY I GO OUT TO SWIM?

Mother, may I go out to swim?
Yes, my darling daughter.
Hang your clothes on a hickory limb
And don't go near the water.

MOSES SUPPOSES
HIS TOESES ARE ROSES

Moses supposes his toeses are roses,
But Moses supposes erroneously;
For nobody's toeses are posies of roses
As Moses supposes his toeses to be.

MRS MASON BOUGHT A BASIN

Mrs Mason bought a basin,
Mrs Tyson said, What a nice 'un,
What did it cost? said Mrs Frost,
Half a crown, said Mrs Brown,
Did it indeed, said Mrs Reed,
It did for certain, said Mrs Burton.
Then Mrs Nix up to her tricks
Threw the basin on the bricks.

Monday's Child

Monday's child is fair of face,
Tuesday's child is full of grace,
Wednesday's child is full of woe,
Thursday's child has far to go,
Friday's child is loving and giving
Saturday's child works hard for its living,
But the child that's born on the Sabbath day
Is bonny and blithe, and good and gay.

Milkman, Milkman

Milkman, milkman; where have you been?
In Buttermilk Channel up to my chin;
I spilt my milk, and I spoilt my clothes,
And got a long icicle hung from my nose.

Matthew, Mark, Luke, and John

Matthew, Mark, Luke, and John,
Hold my horse till I leap on,
Hold him steady, hold him sure,
And I'll get over the misty moor.

The Key Of The Kingdom

This is the key of the kingdom:
In that kingdom is a city,
In that city is a town,
In that town there is a street,
In that street there winds a lane,
In that lane there is a yard,
In that yard there is a house,
In that house there waits a room,
In that room there is a bed,
On that bed there is a basket,
A basket of flowers.

Flowers in the basket,
Basket on the bed,
Bed in the chamber,
Chamber in the house,
House in the weedy yard,
Yard in the winding lane,
Lane in the broad street,
Street in the high town,
Town in the city,
City in the kingdom:
This is the key of the kingdom.

To Market, To Market

To market, to market,
To buy a fat pig;
Home again, home again,
Jiggety jig.

To market, to market,
To buy a fat hog;
Home again, home again,
Jiggety jog.

THIS LITTLE PIG HAD A RUB-A-DUB

This little pig had a rub-a-dub,
This little pig had a scrub-a-scrub,
This little pig-a-wig ran upstairs,
This little pig-a-wig called out, Bears!
Down came the jar with a loud
Slam! Slam!
And this little pig had all the jam.

THIRTY DAYS

Thirty days hath September,
April, June, and November;
All the rest have thirty-one,
Excepting February alone,
And that has twenty-eight days clear
And twenty-nine in each leap year.

THIS LITTLE PIG WENT TO MARKET

This little pig went to market,
This little pig stayed at home;
This little pig had roast beef,
This little pig had none.
This little pig cried, Wee-wee-wee,
I can't find my way home.

THE THREE LITTLE KITTENS

Three little kittens
They lost their mittens,
And they began to cry,
Oh, Mother dear,
We sadly fear
Our mittens we have lost.
What! lost your mittens,
You naughty kittens!
Then you shall have no pie.
Mee-ow, mee-ow, mee-ow.
No, you shall have no pie.

The three little kittens
Put on their mittens
And soon ate up the pie;
Oh, Mother dear,
We greatly fear
Our mittens we have soiled.
What! soiled your mittens,
You naughty kittens!
Then they began to sigh,
Mee-ow, mee-ow, mee-ow,
Then they began to sigh.

The three little kittens
They found their mittens,
And they began to cry,
Oh, Mother dear,
See here, see here,
Our mittens we have found.
Put on your mittens,
You silly kittens,
And you shall have some pie.
Purr-r, purr-r, purr-r,
Oh, let us have some pie.

The three little kittens
They washed their mittens,
And hung them out to dry;
Oh, Mother dear,
Do you not hear,
Our mittens we have washed.
What! washed your mittens,
Then you're good kittens,
But I smell a rat close by,
Mee-ow, mee-ow, mee-ow,
We smell a rat close by.

THREE YOUNG RATS

Three young rats with black felt hats,
Three young ducks with white straw flats,
Three young dogs with curling tails,
Three young cats with demi-veils,
Went out to walk with three young pigs
In satin vests and sorrel wigs;
But suddenly it chanced to rain
And so they all went home again.

TOM, TOM, THE PIPER'S SON

Tom, Tom, the piper's son,
Stole a pig and away he run;
The pig was eat,
And Tom was beat,
And Tom went howling down the street.

THREE LITTLE GHOSTESSES

Three little ghostesses,
Sitting on postesses,
Eating buttered toastesses,
Greasing their fistesses,
Up to their wristesses,
Oh, what beastesses
To make such feastesses!

ELSIE MARLEY

E lsie Marley is grown so fine,
  She won't get up to feed the swine,
But lies in bed till eight or nine,
Lazy Elsie Marley.

FIRE! FIRE!

F ire! Fire! said Mrs Dyer;
  Where? Where? said Mrs Dare;
Up the town, said Mrs Brown;
Any damage? said Mrs Gamage;
None at all, said Mrs Hall.

FEE, FI, FO, FUM

Fee, fi, fo, fum,
I smell the blood of an Englishman:
Be he alive or be he dead,
I'll grind his bones to make my bread.

OLD KING COLE

Old King Cole
Was a merry old soul,
And a merry old soul was he;
He called for his pipe,
And he called for his bowl,
And he called for his fiddlers three.

Every fiddler, he had a fiddle,
And a very fine fiddle had he;
Twee tweedle dee, tweedle dee,
went the fiddlers.
  Oh, there's none so rare
  As can compare
  With King Cole
    and his fiddlers three.

OH, THAT I WERE

Oh, that I were
Where I would be,
Then would I be
Where I am not;
But where I am
There I must be,
And where I would be
I can not.

THE GRAND OLD DUKE OF YORK

Oh, the grand old Duke of York,
He had ten thousand men;
He marched them up to the top of the hill,
And he marched them down again.
And when they were up, they were up,
And when they were down, they were down,
And when they were only half way up,
They were neither up nor down.

OLD FARMER GILES

Old Farmer Giles,
He went seven miles
With his faithful dog Old Rover;
And Old Farmer Giles,
When he came to the stiles,
Took a run, and jumped clean over.

ROCK-A-BYE BABY

Rock-a-bye, baby,
Thy cradle is green,
Father's a nobleman,
Mother's a queen;

And Betty's a lady,
And wears a gold ring;
And Johnny's a drummer,
And drums for the king.

ST DUNSTAN

St Dunstan, as the story goes,
Once pulled the devil by his nose,
With red hot tongs, which made him roar
That could be heard ten miles or more.

ROUND AND ROUND THE GARDEN

Round and round the garden
Went the Teddy Bear,
One step,
Two steps,
Tickly under there.

ROUND AND ROUND
THE RUGGED ROCK

Round and round the rugged rock
The ragged rascal ran.
How many R's are there in that?
Now tell me if you can.

A ROBIN AND A ROBIN'S SON

A robin and a robin's son
Once went to town to buy a bun,
They couldn't decide on plum or plain,
And so they went back home again.

Tom Thumb's Picture Alphabet

A was an archer,
who shot at a frog;

B was a butcher,
and had a great dog.

D was a drunkard,
and had a red face.

C was a captain,
all covered with lace;

F was a farmer,
and followed the plough.

GAMBLING
NEVER PAYS!

E was an esquire,
with pride on his brow;

G was a gamester,
who had but ill-luck;

H was a hunter,
and hunted a buck.

I was an innkeeper,
who loved to carouse;

J was a joiner,
and built up a house.

K was King William,
once governed this land;

L was a lady,
who had a white hand.

M was a miser,
and hoarded up gold;

N was a nobleman,
gallant and bold.

O was an oyster girl,
and went about town;

P was a parson,
and wore a black gown.

Q was a queen,
who wore a silk slip;

R was a robber,
and wanted a whip.

S was a sailor,
and spent all he got;

T was a tinker,
and mended a pot.

U was a usurer,
a miserable elf;

V was a vinter,
who drank all himself.

X was expensive,
and so became poor.

W was a watchman,
and guarded the door;

Y was a youth,
that did not love school;

Z was a zany,
a poor harmless fool.

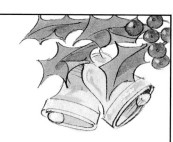

JINGLE BELLS

J ingle, bells! jingle, bells!
Jingle all the way;
Oh, what fun it is to ride
In a one-horse open sleigh.

JOHN BULL

J ohn Bull, John Bull,
Your belly's so full,
You can't jump over
A three-legged stool.

JACK SPRAT

J ack Sprat could eat no fat,
His wife could eat no lean,
And so between them both, you see,
They licked the platter clean.

JEREMIAH OBADIAH

Jeremiah Obadiah, puff, puff, puff.
When he gives his messages he snuffs, snuffs, snuffs,
When he goes to school by day, he roars, roars, roars,
When he goes to bed at night he snores, snores, snores,
When he goes to Christmas treat he eats plum-duff,
Jeremiah Obadiah, puff, puff, puff.

LADYBIRD, LADYBIRD, FLY AWAY HOME

Ladybird, ladybird,
Fly away home,
Your house is on fire
And your children all gone;
All except one
And that's little Ann
And she has crept under
The warming pan.

JERRY HALL

Jerry Hall,
He is so small,
A rat could eat him,
Hat and all.

LUCY LOCKET

Lucy Locket lost her pocket,
Kitty Fisher found it;
Not a penny was there in it,
Only ribbon round it.

ON SATURDAY NIGHT

On Saturday night I lost my wife,
And where do you think I found her?
Up in the moon, singing a tune,
And all the stars around her.

OLD WOMAN, OLD WOMAN

Old woman, old woman,
Shall we go a-shearing?
Speak a little louder, sir,
I'm very thick of hearing.
Old woman, old woman,
Shall I love you dearly?
Thank you very kindly, sir,
Now I hear you clearly.

THE MAN IN THE MOON
LOOKED OUT OF THE MOON

The Man in the Moon looked out of the moon,
Looked out of the moon and said,
'Tis time for all children on the earth
To think about getting to bed!

LITTLE BO-PEEP

Little Bo-peep has lost her sheep,
And doesn't know where to find them;
Leave them alone, and they'll come home,
Bringing their tails behind them.

Little Bo-peep fell fast asleep,
And dreamt she heard them bleating;
But when she awoke, she found it a joke,
For they were still a-fleeting.

Then up she took her little crook,
Determined for to find them;
She found them indeed,
but it made her heart bleed
For they'd left their tails behind them.

It happened one day, as Bo-peep did stray
Into a meadow hard by,
There she espied their tails side by side,
All hung on a tree to dry.

She heaved a sigh, and wiped her eye,
And over the hillocks went rambling,
And tried what she could,
as a shepherdess should.
To tack again each to its lambkin.

LITTLE JACK HORNER

Little Jack Horner
Sat in the corner,
Eating his Christmas pie;
He put in his thumb,
And pulled out a plum,
And said, What a good boy am I!

LITTLE MAN IN COAL PIT

Little man in coal pit
Goes knock, knock, knock;
Up he comes, up he comes,
Out at the top.

MAGPIE, MAGPIE, FLUTTER AND FLEE

Magpie, magpie, flutter and flee,
Turn up your tail and good luck come to me.

I DO NOT LIKE THEE, DOCTOR FELL

I do not like thee, Doctor Fell,
The reason why I cannot tell;
But this I know, and know full well,
I do not like thee, Doctor Fell.

THE MOCKING BIRD

Hush, little baby, don't say a word,
Papa's going to buy you a mocking bird.

If the mocking bird won't sing,
Papa's going to buy you a diamond ring.

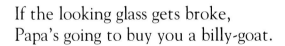

If the diamond ring turns to brass,
Papa's going to buy you a looking glass.

If the looking glass gets broke,
Papa's going to buy you a billy-goat.

If that billy goat runs away,
Papa's going to buy you another today.

I Had A Little Husband

I had a little husband
No bigger than my thumb;
I put him in a pint pot
And there I bade him drum.
I gave him some garters
To garter up his hose,
And a little silk handkerchief
To wipe his pretty nose.

I Am A Pretty Wench

I am a pretty wench,
And I come a great way hence,
And sweethearts I can get none:
But every dirty sow
Can get sweethearts enough,
And I pretty wench can get none.

THE QUEEN OF HEARTS

The Queen of Hearts
She made some tarts,
All on a summer's day;
The Knave of Hearts
He stole those tarts,
And took them clean away.

The King of Hearts
Called for the tarts,
And beat the knave full sore;
The Knave of Hearts
Brought back the tarts,
And vowed he'd steal no more.

RED STOCKINGS, BLUE STOCKINGS

Red stockings, blue stockings,
Shoes tied up with silver;
A red rosette upon my breast
And a gold ring on my finger.

HODDLEY, PODDLEY, PUDDLE AND FOGS

Hoddley, poddley, puddle and fogs,
Cats are to marry the poodle dogs;
Cats in blue jackets and dogs in red hats,
What will become of the mice and the rats?

HIGHER THAN A HOUSE

Higher than a house,
Higher than a tree;
Oh, whatever can that be?

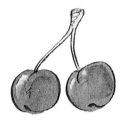

LITTLE NANCY ETTICOAT

Little Nancy Etticoat,
With a white petticoat,
And a red nose;
She has no feet or hands,
The longer she stands
The shorter she grows.

SEE, SEE! WHAT SHALL I SEE?

See, see! what shall I see?
A horse's head where his tail should be!

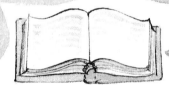

GOES THROUGH THE MUD

Goes through the mud,
And through the mud,
And only leaves one track.

IN SPRING I LOOK GAY

In Spring I look gay,
Decked in comely array,
In Summer more clothing I wear;
When colder it grows,
I fling off my clothes,
And in Winter quite naked appear.

RIDDLE ME REE

Riddle me, riddle me ree,
A little man in a tree;
A stick in his hand,
A stone in his throat,
If you read me this riddle
I'll give you a groat.

HIGHTY TIGHTY, PARADIGHTY

Highty tighty, paradighty,
Clothed all in green,
The king could not read it,
No more could the queen;
They sent for the wise men
From out of the East,
Who said it had horns,
But was not a beast.

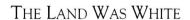

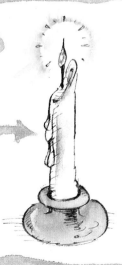

THE LAND WAS WHITE

The land was white,
The seed was black;
It will take a good scholar
To riddle me that.

THE BIG SHIP SAILS
THROUGH THE ALLEY, ALLEY O

The big ship sails through the Alley, Alley O,
Alley, Alley O, Alley, Alley O;
The big ship sails through the Alley, Alley O
On the last day of September.

The Captain said, It will never, never do,
Never, never do, never, never do, etc.

The big ship sank to the bottom of the sea,
The bottom of the sea, the bottom of the sea, etc.

We all dip our heads in the deep blue sea,
The deep blue sea, the deep blue sea, etc.

BLIND MAN, BLIND MAN

Blind man, blind man,
Sure you can't see?
Turn around three times,
And try to catch me.
Turn east, turn west,
Catch as you can,
Did you think you'd caught me?
Blind, blind man!

BOW-WOW

Bow-wow, says the dog,
Mew, mew, says the cat,
Grunt, grunt, goes the hog,
And squeak goes the rat.
Tu-whu, says the owl,
Caw, caw, says the crow,
Quack, quack, says the duck,
And what cuckoos say you know.

BOBBY SHAFTO

Bobby Shafto's gone to sea,
Silver buckles at his knee;
He'll come back and marry me,
Bonny Bobby Shafto.

Bobby Shafto's tall and slim,
He's always dressed so neat and trim,
The ladies they all keek at him,
Bonny Bobby Shafto.

Bobby Shafto's bright and fair,
Combing down his yellow hair,
He's my ain for evermair,
Bonny Bobby Shafto.

Bobby Shafto's getten a bairn
For to dandle in his arm;
In his arm and on his knee,
Bobby Shafto loves me.

HICKORY DICKORY DOCK

Hickory, dickory, dock,
The mouse ran up the clock.
The clock struck one,
The mouse ran down,
Hickory, dickory, dock.

HICKETY, PICKETY

Hickety, pickety, my black hen,
She lays eggs for gentlemen;
Gentlemen come every day
To see what my black hen doth lay.

I SAW A FISHPOND

I saw a fishpond all on fire
I saw a house bow to a squire
I saw a parson twelve feet high
I saw a cottage near the sky
I saw a balloon made of lead
I saw a coffin drop down dead
I saw two sparrows run a race
I saw two horses making lace
I saw a girl just like a cat
I saw a kitten wear a hat
I saw a man who saw these too
And said though strange
they all were true.

THE MILK MAID

Where are you going to, my pretty maid?
I'm going a-milking, sir, she said,
Sir, she said, sir, she said,
I'm going a-milking, sir, she said.

May I go with you, my pretty maid?
You're kindly welcome, sir, she said,
Sir, she said, sir, she said,
You're kindly welcome, sir, she said.

Say, will you marry me, my pretty maid?
Yes, if you please, kind sir, she said,
Sir, she said, sir, she said,
Yes, if you please, kind sir, she said.

What is your father, my pretty maid?
My father's a farmer, sir, she said,
Sir, she said, sir, she said,
My father's a farmer, sir, she said.

What is your fortune, my pretty maid?
My face is my fortune, sir, she said,
Sir, she said, sir, she said,
My face is my fortune, sir, she said.

Then I can't marry you, my pretty maid.
Nobody asked you, sir, she said,
Sir, she said, sir, she said,
Nobody asked you, sir, she said.

THERE WAS A CROOKED MAN

There was a crooked man, and he went a crooked mile,

He found a crooked sixpence beside a crooked stile;

He bought a crooked cat, which caught a crooked mouse,

And they all lived together in a little crooked house.

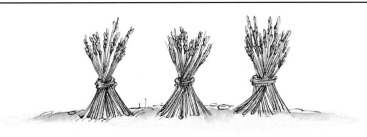

There Was A Jolly Miller

There was a jolly miller and he lived by himself,
As the wheel went round he made his wealth;
With one hand on the hopper and the other on the bag,
As the wheel went round he made his grab.

There Was A Jolly Miller Once

There was a jolly miller once,
Lived on the river Dee;
He worked and sang from morn till night,
No lark more blithe than he.
And this the burden of his song
Forever used to be,
I care for nobody, no! not I,
If nobody cares for me.

PLEASE TO REMEMBER

Please to remember
The Fifth of November,
Gunpowder treason and plot;
I see no reason
Why gunpowder treason
Should ever be forgot.

POLLY PUT THE KETTLE ON

Polly put the kettle on,
Polly put the kettle on,
Polly put the kettle on,
We'll all have tea.

Sukey take it off again,
Sukey take it off again,
Sukey take it off again,
They've all gone away.

46

PUSSY CAT, PUSSY CAT

Pussy cat, pussy cat,
Where have you been?
I've been up to London
To look at the Queen.

Pussy cat, pussy cat,
What did you there?
I frightened a little mouse
Under her chair.

A DILLER, A DOLLAR

A diller, a dollar,
A ten o'clock scholar,
What makes you come so soon?
You used to come at ten o'clock,
But now you come at noon.

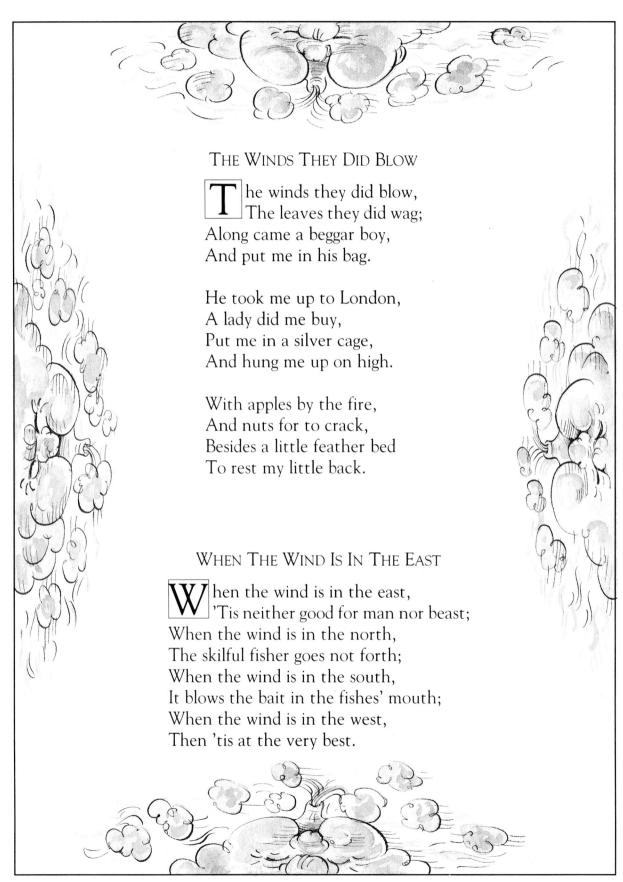

THE WINDS THEY DID BLOW

The winds they did blow,
The leaves they did wag;
Along came a beggar boy,
And put me in his bag.

He took me up to London,
A lady did me buy,
Put me in a silver cage,
And hung me up on high.

With apples by the fire,
And nuts for to crack,
Besides a little feather bed
To rest my little back.

WHEN THE WIND IS IN THE EAST

When the wind is in the east,
'Tis neither good for man nor beast;
When the wind is in the north,
The skilful fisher goes not forth;
When the wind is in the south,
It blows the bait in the fishes' mouth;
When the wind is in the west,
Then 'tis at the very best.

WILLIAM AND MARY

William and Mary,
George and Anne,
Four such children
Had never a man:
They put their father
To flight and shame,
And called their brother
A shocking bad name.

HANNAH BANTRY

Hannah Bantry,
In the pantry,
Gnawing at a mutton bone;
How she gnawed it,
How she clawed it,
When she found herself alone.

THE OWL

A wise old owl sat in an oak,
The more he heard the less he spoke;
The less he spoke the more he heard.
Why aren't we all like that wise old bird?

YANKEE DOODLE

Yankee Doodle came to town,
Riding on a pony;
He stuck a feather in his cap
And called it macaroni.

DICKERY, DICKERY, DARE

Dickery, dickery, dare,
The pig flew up in the air;
The man in brown
Soon brought him down,
Dickery, dickery, dare.

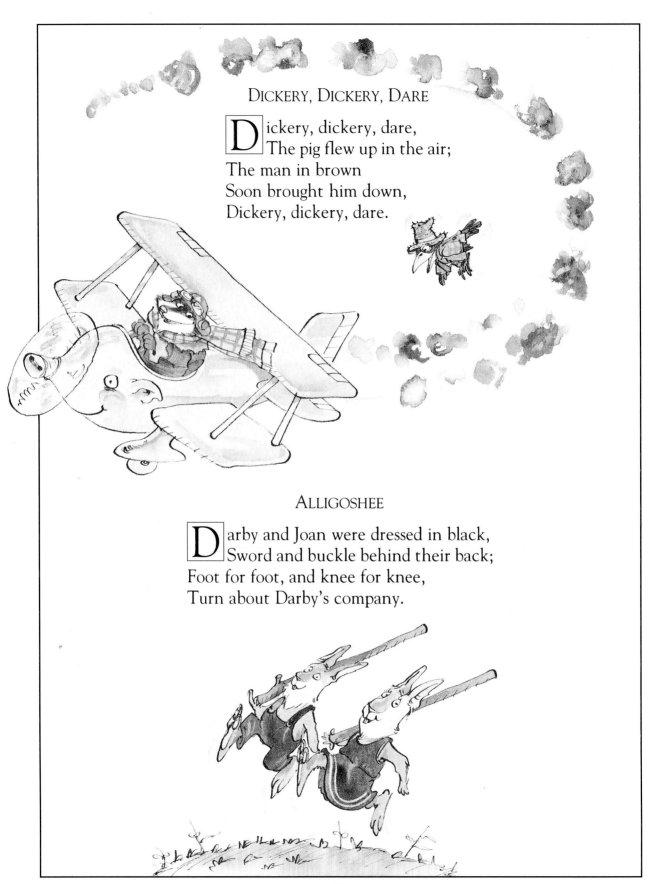

ALLIGOSHEE

Darby and Joan were dressed in black,
Sword and buckle behind their back;
Foot for foot, and knee for knee,
Turn about Darby's company.

DANCE TO YOUR DADDY

Dance to your daddy,
My little babby,
Dance to your daddy, my little lamb;
You shall have a fishy
In a little dishy,
You shall have a fishy when the boat comes in.

DEAR, DEAR! WHAT CAN THE MATTER BE?

Dear, dear! what can the matter be?
Two old women got up in an apple-tree;
One came down, and the other
stayed till Saturday.

CATCH HIM, CROW!

Catch him, crow! carry him, kite!
Take him away till the apples are ripe;
When they are ripe and ready to fall,
Here comes baby, apples, and all.

BRAVE NEWS IS COME TO TOWN

Brave news is come to town,
Brave news is carried;
Brave news is come to town,
Jemmy Dawson's married.

First he got a porridge-pot,
Then he bought a ladle;
Then he got a wife and child,
And then he bought a cradle.

BLOW, WIND, BLOW!

Blow, wind, blow!
And go, mill, go!
That the miller may grind his corn;
That the baker may take it,
And into bread make it,
And bring us a loaf in the morn.

THE BOUGHS DO SHAKE

The boughs do shake and the bells do ring,
So merrily comes our harvest in,
Our harvest in, our harvest in,
So merrily comes our harvest in.

We've ploughed, we've sowed,
We've reaped, we've mowed,
We've got our harvest in.

OLD MOTHER SHUTTLE

Old Mother Shuttle,
Lived in a coal-scuttle
Along with her dog and her cat;
What they ate I can't tell,
But 'tis known very well
That not one of the party was fat.

Old Mother Shuttle
Scoured out her coal-scuttle,
And washed both her dog and her cat;
The cat scratched her nose,
So they came to hard blows,
And who was the gainer by that?

OLD SIR SIMON THE KING

Old Sir Simon the king,
And young Sir Simon the squire,
And old Mrs Hickabout
Kicked Mrs Kickabout
Round about our coal fire.

OH DO YOU KNOW THE MUFFIN MAN

Oh do you know the Muffin Man,
The Muffin Man, the Muffin Man,
Oh do you know the Muffin Man,
Who lives in Drury Lane?

Oh yes, I know the Muffin Man,
The Muffin Man, the Muffin Man,
Oh yes, I know the Muffin Man,
Who lives in Drury Lane.

CHARLEY BARLEY

Charley Barley, butter and eggs,
Sold his wife for three duck eggs.
When the ducks began to lay
Charley Barley flew away.

CHARLEY, CHARLEY

Charley, Charley, stole the barley
Out of the baker's shop,
The baker came out and gave him a clout,
Which made poor Charley hop.

CHARLIE WARLIE

Charlie Warlie had a cow,
Black and white about the brow;
Open the gate and let her through,
Charlie Warlie's old cow.

CHARLIE WAG

Charlie Wag,
Charlie Wag,
Ate the pudding
And left the bag.

ALL WORK AND NO PLAY

All work and no play makes Jack a dull boy;
All play and no work makes Jack a mere toy.

CACKLE, CACKLE, MOTHER GOOSE

Cackle, cackle, Mother Goose,
Have you any feathers loose?
Truly have I, pretty fellow,
Half enough to fill a pillow.
Here are quills, take one or two,
And down to make a bed for you.

A-HUNTING WE WILL GO

A-hunting we will go,
A-hunting we will go;
We'll catch a fox
And put him in a box,
And never let him go.

WHEN I WAS A LITTLE GIRL

When I was a little girl,
About seven years old,
I hadn't got a petticoat,
To keep me from the cold.

So I went into Darlington,
That pretty little town,
And there I bought a petticoat,
A cloak, and a gown.

I went into the woods
And built me a kirk,
And all the birds of the air,
They helped me to work.

The hawk, with his long claws,
Pulled down the stone;
The dove with her rough bill,
Brought me them home.

The parrot was the clergyman,
The peacock was the clerk,
The bullfinch played the organ,
And we made merry work.

WHEN I WAS A LITTLE BOY

When I was a little boy
I had but little wit;
'Tis a long time ago,
And I have no more yet;
Nor ever, ever shall,
Until that I die,
For the longer I live
The more fool am I.

WHO MADE THE PIE?

Who made the pie?
I did.
Who stole the pie?
He did.
Who found the pie?
She did.
Who ate the pie?
You did.
Who cried for pie?
We all did.

When Good King Arthur Ruled This Land

When good King Arthur ruled this land,
He was a goodly King;
He stole three pecks of barley-meal
To make a bag-pudding.

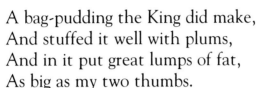

A bag-pudding the King did make,
And stuffed it well with plums,
And in it put great lumps of fat,
As big as my two thumbs.

The King and Queen did eat thereof,
And noblemen beside;
And what they could not eat that night,
The Queen next morning fried.

When Jacky's a Good Boy

When Jacky's a good boy,
He shall have cakes and custard;
But when he does nothing but cry,
He shall have nothing but mustard.

Higglety, Pigglety, Pop!

Higglety, pigglety, pop!
The dog has eaten the mop;
The pig's in a hurry,
The cat's in a flurry,
Higglety, pigglety, pop!

THE TAILOR OF BICESTER

The tailor of Bicester,
He has but one eye;
He cannot cut a pair of green galligaskins,
If he were to die.

THERE WAS A LITTLE GIRL

There was a little girl, and she had a little curl
Right in the middle of her forehead;
When she was good she was very, very good,
But when she was bad she was horrid.

THERE WAS A LITTLE BOY

There was a little boy went into a barn,
And lay down on some hay;
An owl came out and flew about,
And the little boy ran away.

SIX LITTLE MICE SAT DOWN TO SPIN

Six little mice sat down to spin;
Pussy passed by and she peeped in.
What are you doing, my little men?
Weaving coats for gentlemen.
Shall I come in and cut off your threads?
No, no, Mistress Pussy, you'd bite off our heads.
Oh, no, I'll not; I'll help you to spin.
That may be so, but you don't come in.

THE LADY AND THE SWINE

T here was a lady loved a swine,
Honey, quoth she,
Pig-hog wilt thou be mine?
Hoogh, quoth he.

Pinned with a silver pin,
Honey, quoth she,
That thou may go out and in.
Hoogh, quoth he.

I'll build thee a silver sty,
Honey, quoth she,
And in it thou shalt lie.
Hoogh, quoth he.

Wilt thou have me now,
Honey? quoth she.
Speak or my heart will break.
Hoogh, quoth he.

TERENCE MCDIDDLER

T erence McDiddler,
The three-stringed fiddler,
Can charm, if you please,
The fish from the seas.

BOYS AND GIRLS

What are little boys made of, made of?
What are little boys made of?
Frogs and snails
And puppy-dogs' tails,
That's what little boys are made of.

What are little girls made of, made of?
What are little girls made of?
Sugar and spice
And all things nice,
That's what little girls are made of.

WHAT'S THE NEWS?

What's the news of the day,
Good neighbour, I pray?
They say the balloon
Is gone up to the moon.

WEE WILLIE WINKIE

Wee Willie Winkie runs through the town,
Upstairs and downstairs, in his nightgown,
Rapping at the window, crying through the lock:
Are the children in their beds, for it's past eight
o'clock.

THE FAIR MAID WHO, THE FIRST OF MAY

The fair maid who, the First of May,
Goes to the fields at break of day,
And washes in dew from the hawthorn tree,
Will ever after handsome be.

POP GOES THE WEASEL!

Up and down the City Road,
In and out the Eagle,
That's the way the money goes,
Pop goes the weasel!

Half a pound of tuppenny rice,
Half a pound of treacle,
Mix it up and make it nice,
Pop goes the weasel!

Every night when I go out
The monkey's on the table;
Take a stick and knock it off,
Pop goes the weasel!

UP AT PICCADILLY

Up at Piccadilly oh!
The coachman takes his stand,
And when he meets a pretty girl,
He takes her by the hand;
Whip away for ever oh!
Drive away so clever oh!
All the way to Bristol oh!
He drives her four-in-hand.

There Was An Old Woman Tossed Up In A Basket

There was an old woman tossed up in a basket,
Seventeen times as high as the moon;
Where she was going I couldn't but ask it,
For in her hand she carried a broom.

Old woman, old woman, old woman, quoth I,
Where are you going to up so high?
To brush the cobwebs off the sky!
May I go with you? Aye, by-and-by.

There Was A Rat

There was a rat, for want of stairs,
Went down a rope to say his prayers.

The Cats Of Kilkenny

There were once two cats of Kilkenny.
Each thought there was one cat too many;
So they fought and they fit,
And they scratched and they bit,
Till, excepting their nails,
And the tips of their tails,
Instead of two cats, there weren't any.

There Was An Old Woman
Who Lived In A Shoe

There was an old woman who lived in a shoe,
She had so many children she didn't know what
to do;
She gave them some broth without any bread;
She whipped them all soundly and put them to bed.

OLD MOTHER HUBBARD

Old Mother Hubbard
Went to the cupboard,
To fetch her poor dog a bone;
But when she got there
The cupboard was bare
And so the poor dog had none.

She went to the baker's
To buy him some bread;
But when she came back
The poor dog was dead.

She went to the undertaker's
To buy him a coffin;
But when she came back
The poor dog was laughing.

She took a clean dish
To get him some tripe;
But when she came back
He was smoking a pipe.

She went to the fishmonger's
To buy him some fish;
But when she came back
He was licking the dish.

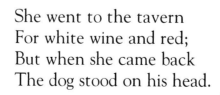

She went to the tavern
For white wine and red;
But when she came back
The dog stood on his head.

She went to the fruiterer's
To buy him some fruit;
But when she came back
He was playing the flute.

She went to the tailor's
To buy him a coat;
But when she came back
He was riding a goat.

She went to the hatter's
To buy him a hat;
But when she came back
He was feeding the cat.

She went to the barber's
To buy him a wig;
But when she came back
He was dancing a jig.

She went to the cobbler's
To buy him some shoes;
But when she came back
He was reading the news.

She went to the seamstress
To buy him some linen;
But when she came back
The dog was a-spinning.

She went to the hosier's
To buy him some hose;
But when she came back
He was dressed in his clothes.

The dame made a curtsey,
The dog made a bow;
The dame said, Your servant,
The dog said, Bow-wow.

BESSY BELL AND MARY GRAY

Bessy Bell and Mary Gray,
They were two bonny lasses;
They built their house upon the lea,
And covered it with rashes.

Bessy kept the garden gate,
And Mary kept the pantry:
Bessy always had to wait,
While Mary lived in plenty.

BETTY BOTTER BOUGHT SOME BUTTER

Betty Botter bought some butter,
But, she said, the butter's bitter;
If I put it in my batter
It will make my batter bitter,
But a bit of better butter,
That would make my batter better.
So she bought a bit of butter,
Better then her bitter butter,
And she put it in her batter
And the batter was not bitter.
So t'was better Betty Botter
Bought a bit of better butter.

COCK A DOODLE DOO

Cock a doodle doo!
My dame has lost her shoe,
My master's lost his fiddling stick
And knows not what to do.

Cock a doodle doo!
What is my dame to do?
Till master finds his fiddling stick
She'll dance without her shoe.

Cock a doodle doo!
My dame has found her shoe,
And master's found his fiddling stick,
Sing doodle doodle doo.

Cock a doodle doo!
My dame will dance with you,
While master fiddles his fiddling stick
For dame and doodle doo.

COBBLER, COBBLER

Cobbler, cobbler, mend my shoe,
Get it done by half past two;
Stitch it up, and stitch it down,
Then I'll give you half a crown.

I SAY THAT'S NOT VERY LONG!

ELIZABETH, ELSPETH, BETSY, AND BESS

Elizabeth, Elspeth, Betsy, and Bess,
They all went together to seek a bird's nest.
They found a bird's nest with five eggs in,
They all took one and left four in.

DOWN BY THE RIVER

Down by the river
Where the green grass grows
Pretty Polly Perkins
Bleaches her clothes.
She laughs and she sings,
And she sings so sweet,
She calls, Come over,
Across the street.
He kissed her, he kissed her,
He took her to the town;
He bought her a ring
And a damascene gown.

THE COCK CROWS IN THE MORN

The cock crows in the morn
To tell us to rise,
And he that lies late
Will never be wise:
For early to bed,
And early to rise,
Is the way to be healthy
And wealthy and wise.

THE DOVE SAYS COO, COO

The dove says, coo, coo,
What shall I do?
I can scarce maintain two.
Pooh, pooh, says the wren,
I have ten,
And keep them all like gentlemen.
Curr dhoo, curr dhoo,
Love me, and I'll love you.

DOWN WITH THE LAMBS

Down with the lambs
Up with the lark,
Run to bed children
Before it gets dark.

THE TWELVE DAYS
OF CHRISTMAS

The first day of Christmas
My true love sent to me
A partridge in a pear tree.

The second day of Christmas
My true love sent to me
Two turtle doves, and
A partridge in a pear tree.

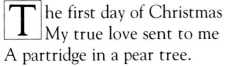

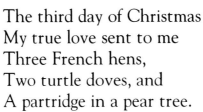

The third day of Christmas
My true love sent to me
Three French hens,
Two turtle doves, and
A partridge in a pear tree.

The fourth day of Christmas
My true love sent to me
Four colly birds,

Three French hens,
Two turtle doves, and
A partridge in a pear tree.

The fifth day of Christmas
My true love sent to me
Five gold rings,
Four colly birds,
Three French hens,
Two turtle doves, and
A partridge in a pear tree.

The sixth day of Christmas
My true love sent to me
Six geese a-laying
Five gold rings,
Four colly birds,
Three French hens,
Two turtle doves, and
A partridge in a pear tree.

The seventh day of Christmas
My true love sent to me
Seven swans a-swimming,
Six geese a-laying,
Five gold rings,
Four colly birds,
Three French hens,
Two turtle doves, and
A partridge in a pear tree.

The eighth day of Christmas
My true love sent to me
Eight maids a-milking,
Seven swans a-swimming,
Six geese a-laying,
Five gold rings,
Four colly birds,
Three French hens,
Two turtle doves, and
A partridge in a pear tree.

The ninth day of Christmas
My true love sent to me
Nine drummers drumming,
Eight maids a-milking,
Seven swans a-swimming,
Six geese a-laying,
Five gold rings,
Four colly birds,
Three French hens,
Two turtle doves, and
A partridge in a pear tree.

The tenth day of Christmas
My true love sent to me
Ten pipers piping
Nine drummers drumming,
Eight maids a-milking,
Seven swans a-swimming,
Six geese a-laying,
Five gold rings,
Four colly birds,
Three French hens,
Two turtle doves, and
A partridge in a pear tree.

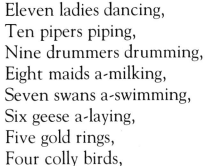

The eleventh day of Christmas
My true love sent to me
Eleven ladies dancing,
Ten pipers piping,
Nine drummers drumming,
Eight maids a-milking,
Seven swans a-swimming,
Six geese a-laying,
Five gold rings,
Four colly birds,
Three French hens,
Two turtle doves, and
A partridge in a pear tree.

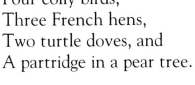

The twelfth day of Christmas
My true love sent to me
Twelve lords a-leaping,
Eleven ladies dancing,
Ten pipers piping,
Nine drummers drumming,
Eight maids a-milking,
Seven swans a-swimming,
Six geese a-laying,
Five gold rings,
Four colly birds,
Three French hens,
Two turtle doves, and
A partridge in a pear tree.

SING A SONG OF SIXPENCE

Sing a song of sixpence,
A pocket full of rye;
Four and twenty blackbirds,
Baked in a pie.

When the pie was opened,
The birds began to sing,
Was not that a dainty dish,
To set before a king?

The king was in his counting-house
Counting out his money;
The queen was in the parlour
Eating bread and honey.

The maid was in the garden,
Hanging out the clothes,
When down came a blackbird
And pecked off her nose.

OUCH!

HOW MANY MILES TO BABYLON?

H ow many miles to Babylon?
Three-score and ten.
Can I get there by candle-light?
Yes, and back again.
If your heels are nimble and light,
You may get there by candle-light.

HUMPTY DUMPTY

H umpty Dumpty sat on a wall,
Humpty Dumpty had a great fall;
All the King's horses and all the King's men
Couldn't put Humpty together again.

LITTLE BLUE BEN

Little Blue Ben, who lives in the glen,
Keeps a blue cat and one blue hen,
Which lays of blue eggs a score and ten;
Where shall I find the little Blue Ben?

HUSH-A-BYE BABY

Hush-a-bye, baby, on the tree top,
When the wind blows the cradle will rock;
When the bough breaks the cradle will fall,
Down will come baby, cradle, and all.

HERE'S TO THEE, OLD APPLE TREE

Here's to thee, old apple tree,
Whence thou may'st bud
And whence thou may'st blow,
And whence thou may'st bear apples enow;
Hats full and caps full,
Bushels full and sacks full,
And our pockets full too.

I SAW THREE SHIPS

I saw three ships come sailing by,
Sailing by, sailing by,
I saw three ships come sailing by,
On New Year's day in the morning.

And what do you think was in them then,
In them then, in them then?
And what do you think was in them then,
On New Year's day in the morning?

Three pretty girls were in them then,
In them then, in them then,
Three pretty girls were in them then,
On New Year's day in the morning.

And one could whistle, and one could sing,
And one could play on the violin,
Such joy there was at my wedding,
On New Year's day in the morning.

I SAW A SHIP A-SAILING

I saw a ship a-sailing,
A-sailing on the sea,
And oh, but it was laden
With pretty things for thee!

There were comfits in the cabin,
And apples in the hold;
The sails were made of silk,
And the masts were all of gold.

The four-and-twenty sailors
That stood between the decks,
Were four-and-twenty white mice
With chains about their necks.

The captain was a duck
With a packet on his back,
And when the ship began to move
The captain said, Quack! Quack!

As I Was Going To Sell My Eggs

As I was going to sell my eggs,
I met a man with bandy legs;
Bandy legs and crooked toes,
I tripped up his heels and he fell on his nose.

THERE WAS NO NEED FOR THAT YOUNG LADY!

As I Was Going Up Pippen Hill

As I was going up Pippen Hill
Pippen Hill was dirty.
There I met a pretty miss
And she dropt me a curtsey.

Little miss, pretty miss,
Blessings light upon you!
If I had half a crown a day,
I'd spend it all upon you.

As I Went Over Lincoln Bridge

As I went over Lincoln Bridge,
I met Mister Rusticap;
Pins and needles on his back,
A-going to Thorney fair.

BOYS AND GIRLS COME OUT TO PLAY

Boys and girls come out to play,
The moon doth shine as bright as day.
Leave your supper and leave your sleep,
And join your playfellows in the street.
Come with a whoop and come with a call,
Come with a good will or not at all.
Up the ladder and down the wall,
A half-penny loaf will serve us all;
You find milk, and I'll find flour,
And we'll have a pudding in half an hour.

AS I WAS GOING O'ER LONDON BRIDGE

As I was going o'er London Bridge,
I heard something crack;
Not a man in all England
Can mend that.

AS I WENT OVER THE WATER

As I went over the water,
The water went over me.
I saw two little blackbirds
Sitting on a tree;
One called me a rascal,
And one called me a thief,
I took up my little black stick
And knocked out all their teeth.

THE DERBY RAM

As I was going to Derby
Upon a market day,
I met the finest ram, sir,
That ever was fed on hay.

This ram was fat behind, sir,
This ram was fat before,
This ram was three yards high, sir,
Indeed he was no more.

The wool upon his back, sir,
Reached up unto the sky,
The eagles built their nests there,
For I heard the young ones cry.

The wool upon his tail, sir,
Was three yards and an ell,
Of it they made a rope, sir,
To pull the parish bell.

The space between the horns, sir,
Was as far as man could reach,
And there they built a pulpit,
But no one in it preached.

This ram had four legs to walk upon,
This ram had four legs to stand,
And every leg he had, sir,
Stood on an acre of land.

Now the man that fed the ram, sir,
He fed him twice a day,
And each time that he fed him, sir,
He ate a rick of hay.

As I Was Going To St Ives

As I was going to St Ives, I met a man with seven wives;

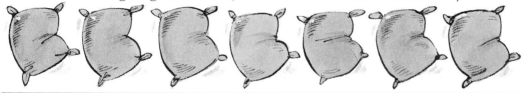

Each wife had seven sacks,

Each sack had seven cats,

Each cat had seven kits:
Kits, cats, sacks, and wives, How many were going to St Ives?

THERE WAS AN OLD WOMAN

There was an old woman
Lived under a hill,
And if she's not gone
She lives there still.

THE PIPER'S COW

There was a piper had a cow,
And he had nought to give her;
He pulled out his pipe, and played her a tune,
And bade the cow consider.

The cow considered very well,
And gave the piper a penny,
And bade him play the other tune –
"Corn rigs are bonny."

There Was An Old Woman Lived Under A Hill

There was an old woman
Lived under a hill,
She put a mouse in a bag,
And sent it to mill;
The miller did swear
By the point of his knife,
He never took toll
Of a mouse in his life!

There Was A Man Of Thessaly

There was a man of Thessaly
And he was wondrous wise,
He jumped into a bramble bush
And scratched out both his eyes.
And when he saw his eyes were out,
With all his might and main
He jumped into another bush
And scratched them in again.

I'll Tell You A Story

I'll tell you a story
About Jack-a-Nory,
And now my story's begun;
I'll tell you another
Of Jack and his brother,
And now my story is done.

If I Had A Donkey

If I had a donkey that wouldn't go,
Would I beat him? Oh no, no.
I'd put him in the barn and give him some corn.
The best little donkey that ever was born.

If Wishes Were Horses

If wishes were horses,
beggars would ride.
If turnips were watches,
I would wear one by my side.

I'm A Little Teapot

I'm a little teapot, short and stout;
Here's my handle, here's my spout.
When I see the tea-cups, hear me shout,
Tip me up and pour me out.

I SEE THE MOON

I see the moon,
And the moon sees me;
God bless the moon,
And God bless me.

I SENT A LETTER TO MY LOVE

I sent a letter to my love
And on the way I dropped it;
One of you has picked it up
And put it in your pocket.

I WENT UP THE HIGH HILL

I went up the high hill,
There I saw a climbing goat;
I went down by the running rill,
There I saw a ragged sheep;
I went out to the roaring sea,
There I saw a tossing boat;
I went under the green tree,
There I saw two doves asleep.

LITTLE TOMMY TITTLEMOUSE

Little Tommy Tittlemouse
Lived in a little house;
He caught fishes
In other men's ditches.

DIDDLE, DIDDLE, DUMPLING

Diddle, diddle, dumpling, my son John,
Went to bed with his trousers on;
One shoe off, and one shoe on,
Diddle, diddle, dumpling, my son John.

Little Miss Muffet

Little Miss Muffet
Sat on a tuffet,
Eating her curds and whey;
There came a big spider,
Who sat down beside her
And frightened Miss Muffet away.

As I Went To Bonner

As I went to Bonner,
I met a pig
Without a wig,
Upon my word and honour.

NEEDLES AND PINS

Needles and pins, needles and pins,
When a man marries his trouble begins.

MARCH WINDS

March winds and April showers
Bring forth May flowers.

THE NORTH WIND DOTH BLOW

The north wind doth blow,
And we shall have snow,
And what will poor Robin do then,
Poor thing?
He'll sit in a barn,
And keep himself warm,
And hide his head under his wing,
Poor thing.

NOSE, NOSE

Nose, nose, jolly red nose,
And what gave thee that jolly red nose?
Nutmeg and ginger, cinnamon and cloves,
That's what gave me this jolly red nose.

NOW WHAT DO YOU THINK

Now what do you think
Of little Jack Jingle?
Before he was married
He used to live single.
But after he married,
To alter his life,
He left off living single
And lived with his wife.

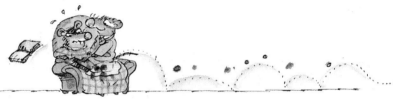

MY LITTLE OLD MAN AND I FELL OUT

My little old man and I fell out
How shall we bring this matter about?
Bring it about as well as you can,
And get you gone, you little old man!

HERE WE GO ROUND THE MULBERRY BUSH

Here we go round the mulberry bush,
The mulberry bush, the mulberry bush,
Here we go round the mulberry bush,
On a cold and frosty morning.

This is the way we wash our hands,
Wash our hands, wash our hands,
This is the way we wash our hands,
On a cold and frosty morning.

This is the way we wash our clothes,
Wash our clothes, wash our clothes,
This is the way we wash our clothes,
On a cold and frosty morning.

This is the way we go to school,
Go to school, go to school,
This is the way we go to school,
On a cold and frosty morning.

This is the way we come out of school,
Come out of school, come out of school,
This is the way we come out of school,
On a cold and frosty morning.

HERE'S SULKY SUE

Here's Sulky Sue;
What shall we do?
Turn her face to the wall
Till she comes to.

HIE TO THE MARKET

Hie to the market, Jenny come trot,
Spilt all her butter milk, every drop,
Every drop and every dram,
Jenny came home with an empty can.

ADVICE

He that would thrive
Must rise at five;
He that hath thriven
May lie till seven;
He that will never thrive
May lie till eleven.

SIMPLE SIMON

Simple Simon met a pieman
Going to the fair;
Says Simple Simon to the pieman,
Let me taste your ware.

Says the pieman to Simple Simon,
Show me first your penny;
Says Simple Simon to the pieman,
Indeed I have not any.

Simple Simon went a-fishing,
For to catch a whale;
All the water he had got
Was in his mother's pail.

Simple Simon went a-hunting,
For to catch a hare;
He rode a goat about the streets,
But couldn't find one there.

He went to catch a dickey bird,
And thought he could not fail,
Because he'd got a little salt,
To put upon its tail.

He went to shoot a wild duck,
But wild duck flew away;
Says Simon, I can't hit him,
Because he will not stay.

He went to ride a spotted cow,
That had a little calf;
She threw him down upon the ground,
Which made the people laugh.

Once Simon made a great snowball,
And brought it in to roast;
He laid it down before the fire,
And soon the ball was lost.

He went to try if cherries ripe
Did grow upon a thistle;
He pricked his finger very much
Which made poor Simon whistle.

He went for water in a sieve,
But soon it all ran through;
And now poor Simple Simon
Bids you all adieu.

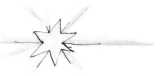

TWINKLE, TWINKLE, LITTLE STAR

Twinkle, twinkle, little star,
How I wonder what you are!
Up above the world so high,
Like a diamond in the sky.

TWEEDLEDUM AND TWEEDLEDEE

Tweedledum and Tweedledee
Agreed to have a battle,
For Tweedledum said Tweedledee
Had spoiled his nice new rattle.
Just then flew by a monstrous crow
As black as a tar-barrel,
Which frightened both the heroes so,
They quite forgot their quarrel.

Two Little Dogs

Two little dogs
Sat by the fire
Over a fender of coal-dust;
Said one little dog
To the other little dog,
If you don't talk, why, I must.

Two Little Dicky-Birds

Two little dicky-birds
Sitting on a wall,
One named Peter, one named Paul.
Fly away Peter, fly away Paul;
Come back Peter,
Come back Paul.

H ey diddle, diddle,
The cat and the fiddle,

The cow jumped over the moon;

The little dog laughed
To see such sport,

And the dish ran away with the spoon.

LITTLE BOY BLUE

Little Boy Blue,
Come blow up your horn,
The sheep's in the meadow,
The cow's in the corn.
Where is the boy
Who looks after the sheep?
He's under a haystack
Fast asleep.
Will you wake him?
No, not I,
For if I do,
He's sure to cry.

OH THE LITTLE RUSTY DUSTY MILLER

Oh the little rusty dusty miller,
Dusty was his coat,
Dusty was his colour,
Dusty was the kiss
I got from the miller.
If I had my pockets
Full of gold and siller,
I would give it all
To my dusty miller.

BRING DADDY HOME

Bring Daddy home
With a fiddle and a drum,
A pocket full of spices,
An apple and a plum.

RIDE A COCK HORSE

Ride a cock horse
To Banbury Cross,
To see a fine lady
Upon a white horse.
With rings on her fingers
And bells on her toes,
She shall have music
Wherever she goes.

RATS IN THE GARDEN

Rats in the garden, catch 'em Towser,
Cows in the cornfield, run, boys, run;
Cat's in the cream pot, stop her, now sir,
Fire on the mountain, run, boys, run.

QUEEN CAROLINE

Queen, Queen Caroline,
Washed her hair in turpentine,
Turpentine to make it shine,
Queen, Queen Caroline.

Ring O' Roses

Ring a ring o' roses,
A pocket full of posies,
A-tishoo, a-tishoo,
We all fall down.

I'm The King Of The Castle

I'm the king of the castle,
Get down you dirty rascal.

THE LION AND THE UNICORN

The lion and the unicorn
Were fighting for the crown;
The lion beat the unicorn
All around the town.

Some gave them white bread,
And some gave them brown;
Some gave them plum cake
And drummed them out of town.

LITTLE JACK DANDY-PRAT

Little Jack Dandy-prat
Was my first suitor;
He had a dish and spoon
And a little pewter;
He'd linen and woollen,
And woollen and linen,
A little pig on a string
Cost him five shilling.

LAVENDER'S BLUE

Lavender's blue, diddle, diddle,
Lavender's green;
When I am king, diddle, diddle,
You shall be queen.

Call up your men, diddle, diddle,
Set them to work,
Some to the plough, diddle, diddle,
Some to the cart.

Some to make hay, diddle, diddle,
Some to thresh corn,
Whilst you and I, diddle, diddle,
Keep ourselves warm.

LITTLE GIRL

Little girl, little girl,
Where have you been?
I've been to see grandmother
Over the green.
What did she give you?
Milk in a can.
What did you say for it?
Thank you, Grandam.

LILIES ARE WHITE

Lilies are white,
Rosemary's green,
When I am king,
You shall be queen.

LITTLE BETTY BLUE

Little Betty Blue
Lost her holiday shoe,
What shall little Betty do?
Buy her another
To match the other,
And then she'll walk upon two.

GO TO BED LATE

Go to bed late,
Stay very small;
Go to bed early,
Grow very tall.

FIRST IN A CARRIAGE

First in a carriage,
Second in a gig,
Third on a donkey,
And fourth on a pig.

GEORGIE PORGIE

Georgie Porgie, pudding and pie,
Kissed the girls and made them cry;
When the boys came out to play,
Georgie Porgie ran away.

FOUR AND TWENTY TAILORS

Four and twenty tailors went to kill a snail,
The best man amongst them durst not touch her tail;
She put out her horns like a little Kyloe cow,
Run, tailors, run, or she'll kill you all e'en now.

GINGER, GINGER

Ginger, Ginger, broke the winder,
Hit the winder – Crack!
The baker came out to give 'im a clout
And landed on 'is back.

THE HORSESHOE NAIL

For want of a nail the shoe was lost,
For want of a shoe the horse was lost,
For want of a horse the rider was lost,
For want of a rider the battle was lost,
For want of a battle the kingdom was lost,
And all for the want of a horseshoe nail.

GOOD NIGHT

Good night, sweet repose,
Half the bed and all the clothes.

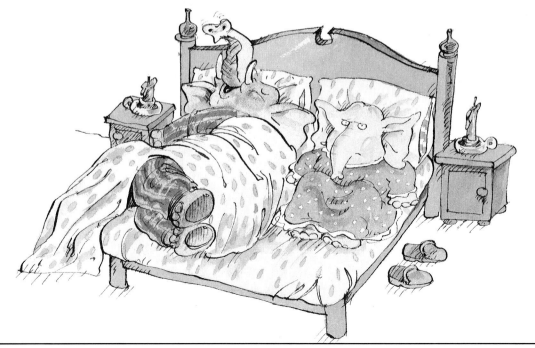

PETER WHITE WILL NE'ER GO RIGHT

Peter White will ne'er go right;
Would you know the reason why?
He follows his nose wherever he goes,
And that stands all awry.

PAT-A-CAKE, PAT-A-CAKE

Pat-a-cake, pat-a-cake,
Baker's man,
Bake me a cake
As fast as you can.
Pat it and prick it
And mark it with B,
And bake in the oven
For Baby and me.

PEASE PORRIDGE HOT

Pease porridge hot,
Pease porridge cold,
Pease porridge in the pot
Nine days old.
Some like it hot,
Some like it cold,
Some like it in the pot
Nine days old.

PETER PIPER

Peter Piper picked a peck of pickled pepper;
A peck of pickled pepper Peter Piper picked.
If Peter Piper picked a peck of pickled pepper,
Where's the peck of pickled pepper Peter Piper picked?

PETER, PETER, PUMPKIN EATER

Peter, Peter, pumpkin eater,
Had a wife and couldn't keep her;
He put her in a pumpkin shell
And there he kept her very well.

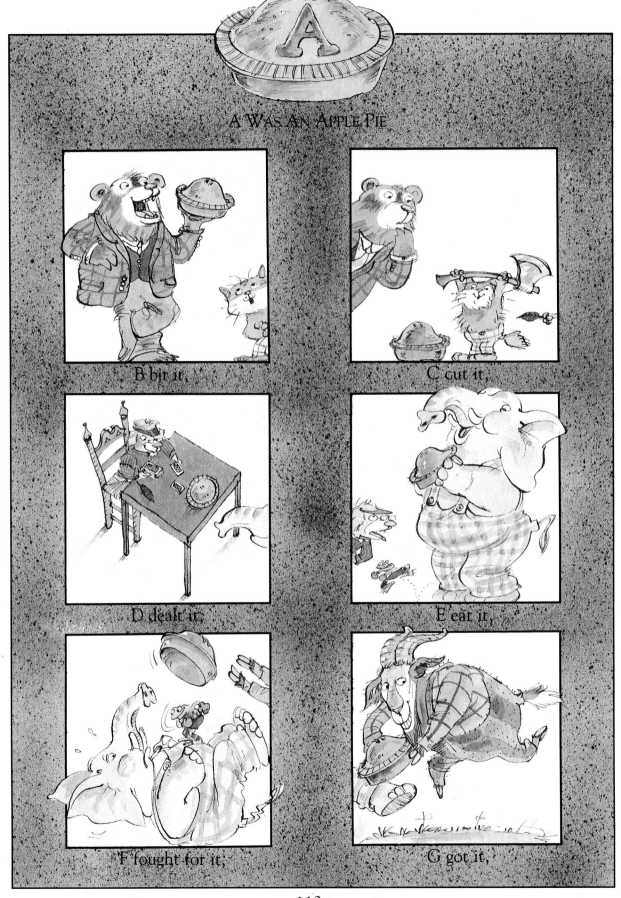

A WAS AN APPLE PIE

B bit it,

C cut it,

D dealt it,

E eat it,

F fought for it,

G got it,

H had it,

I inspected it,

J jumped for it,

K kept it,

L longed for it,

M mourned for it,

N nodded at it,

O opened it,

P peeped in it,,

Q quartered it,

R ran for it,

S stole it,

T took it,

U upset it,

V viewed it,

W wanted it,

X, Y, Z, and ampersand
All wished for a piece in hand.

I HAD A LITTLE NUT TREE

I had a little nut tree,
Nothing would it bear
But a silver nutmeg
And a golden pear;
The king of Spain's daughter
Came to visit me,
And all for the sake
Of my little nut tree.

I HAD TWO PIGEONS

I had two pigeons bright and gay,
They flew from me the other day;
What was the reason they did go?
I cannot tell for I do not know.

I LOVE LITTLE PUSSY

I love little pussy,
Her coat is so warm,
And if I don't hurt her
She'll do me no harm.
So I'll not pull her tail,
Nor drive her away,
But pussy and I
Very gently will play.
She shall sit by my side,
And I'll give her some food;
And pussy will love me
Because I am good.

I Had A Little Pony

I had a little pony,
His name was Dapple Gray;
I lent him to a lady
To ride a mile away.
She whipped him, she slashed him,
She rode him through the mire;
I would not lend my pony now,
For all the lady's hire.

I Love Sixpence

I love sixpence, jolly little sixpence,
I love sixpence better than my life;
I spent a penny of it, I lent a penny of it,
And I took fourpence home to my wife.

Oh, my little fourpence, jolly little fourpence,
I love fourpence better than my life;
I spent a penny of it, I lent a penny of it,
And I took twopence home to my wife.

Oh, my little twopence, jolly little twopence,
I love twopence better than my life;
I spent a penny of it, I lent a penny of it,
And I took nothing home to my wife.

Oh, my little nothing, jolly little nothing,
What will nothing buy for my wife?
I have nothing, I spend nothing,
I love nothing better than my wife.

THE MAN IN THE MOON

The man in the moon
Came down too soon,
And asked his way to Norwich;
He went by the south,
And burnt his mouth
With supping cold plum porridge.

MARY, MARY, QUITE CONTRARY

Mary, Mary, quite contrary,
How does your garden grow?
With silver bells and cockle shells,
And pretty maids all in a row.

A MAN IN THE WILDERNESS

A man in the wilderness asked me,
How many strawberries grow in the sea,
I answered him, as I thought good,
As many red herrings as swim in the wood.

MARY HAD A LITTLE LAMB

Mary had a little lamb,
Its fleece was white as snow;
And everywhere that Mary went
The lamb was sure to go.
It followed her to school one day,
Which was against the rule;
It made the children laugh and play
To see a lamb at school.
And so the teacher turned it out,
But still it lingered near,
And waited patiently about
Till Mary did appear.
Why does the lamb love Mary so?
The eager children cry;
Why, Mary loves the lamb, you know,
The teacher did reply.

LITTLE TEE-WEE

Little Tee-wee,
He went to sea,
In an open boat;
And when it was afloat,
The little boat bended,
My story's ended.

LITTLE TOMMY TUCKER

Little Tommy Tucker
Sings for his supper:
What shall we give him?
White bread and butter.
How shall he cut it
Without e'er a knife?
How will he be married
Without e'er a wife?

THE HOUSE THAT JACK BUILT

This is the house that Jack built.

This is the malt
That lay in the house
that Jack built.

This is the rat,
That ate the malt
That lay in the house
that Jack built.

This is the cat,
That killed the rat,
That ate the malt
That lay in the house
that Jack built.

This is the dog,
That worried the cat,
That killed the rat,
That ate the malt
That lay in the house
that Jack built.

This is the cow
with the crumpled horn,
That tossed the dog,
That worried the cat,
That killed the rat,
That ate the malt
That lay in the house
that Jack built.

This is the maiden
all forlorn,
That milked the cow
with the crumpled horn,
That tossed the dog,
That worried the cat
That killed the rat,
That ate the malt
That lay in the house
that Jack built.

This is the man all tattered and torn,
That kissed the maiden all forlorn,
That milked the cow with the crumpled horn,
That tossed the dog,
That worried the cat,
That killed the rat,
That ate the malt
That lay in the house that Jack built.

This is the priest all shaven and shorn,
That married the man all tattered and torn,
That kissed the maiden all forlorn,
That milked the cow with the crumpled horn,
That tossed the dog,
That worried the cat,
That killed the rat,
That ate the malt
That lay in the house that Jack built.

This is the cock that crowed in the morn,
That waked the priest all shaven and shorn,
That married the man all tattered and torn,
That kissed the maiden all forlorn,
That milked the cow with the crumpled horn,
That tossed the dog,
That worried the cat,
That killed the rat,
That ate the malt
That lay in the house that Jack built.

This is the farmer sowing his corn,
That kept the cock that crowed in the morn,
That waked the priest all shaven and shorn,
That married the man all tattered and torn,
That kissed the maiden all forlorn,
That milked the cow with the crumpled horn,
That tossed the dog,
That worried the cat,
That killed the rat,
That ate the malt
That lay in the house that Jack built.

This is the horse and the hound and the horn,
That belonged to the farmer sowing his corn,
That kept the cock that crowed in the morn,
That waked the priest all shaven and shorn,
That married the man all tattered and torn,
That kissed the maiden all forlorn,
That milked the cow with the crumpled horn,
That tossed the dog, That worried the cat,
That killed the rat, That ate the malt
That lay in the house that Jack built.

TICKLY, TICKLY, ON YOUR KNEE

Tickly, tickly, on your knee,
If you laugh you don't love me.

TINKER, TAILOR

Tinker,
Tailor,
Soldier,
Sailor,
Rich man,
Poor man,
Beggar man,
Thief.

TIT, TAT, TOE

Tit, tat, toe,
My first go,
Three jolly butcher boys
All in a row;
Stick one up, stick one down,
Stick one in the old man's crown.

TOMMY TROT

Tommy Trot, a man of law,
Sold his bed and lay upon straw;
Sold the straw and slept on grass,
To buy his wife a looking-glass.

TO SLEEP EASY ALL NIGHT

To sleep easy all night,
Let your supper be light,
Or else you'll complain
Of a stomach in pain.

ROSES ARE RED

Roses are red,
Violets are blue,
Sugar is sweet
And so are you.

Jack And Jill

Jack and Jill
Went up the hill,
To fetch a pail of water;
Jack fell down,
And broke his crown,
And Jill came tumbling after.

Then up Jack got,
And home did trot,
As fast as he could caper;
To old Dame Dob,
Who patched his nob
With vinegar and brown paper.

When Jill came in,
How she did grin
To see Jack's paper plaster;
Her mother, vexed,
Did whip her next,
For laughing at Jack's disaster.

Now Jack did laugh
And Jill did cry,
But her tears did soon abate;
Then Jill did say,
That they should play
At see-saw across the gate.

IT'S ONCE I COURTED AS PRETTY A LASS

I t's once I courted as pretty a lass,
As ever your eyes did see;
But now she's come to such a pass,
She never will do for me.
She invited me to her house,
Where oft I'd been before,
And she tumbled me into the hog-tub,
And I'll never go there any more.

IT'S RAINING

I t's raining, it's pouring,
The old man's snoring;
He got into bed
And bumped his head
And couldn't get up in the morning.

INCEY WINCEY

I ncey Wincey spider
Climbing up the spout;
Down came the rain
And washed the spider out;
Out came the sunshine
And dried up all the rain;
Incey Wincey spider
Climbing up again.

LITTLE ROBIN REDBREAST

L ittle Robin Redbreast sat upon a tree;
Up went Pussy cat and down went he.
Down came Pussy cat, and away Robin ran;
Says little Robin Redbreast, Catch me if you can.

LITTLE KING PIPPIN

Little King Pippin
he built a fine hall,
Pie-crust and pastry-crust
that was the wall;
The windows were made
of black pudding and white,
And slated with pancakes,
you ne'er saw the like.

A LITTLE OLD MAN OF DERBY

A little old man of Derby,
How do you think he served me?
He took away my bread and cheese,
And that is how he served me.

LITTLE POLLY FLINDERS

Little Polly Flinders
Sat among the cinders,
Warming her pretty little toes;
Her mother came and caught her,
And whipped her little daughter
For spoiling her nice new clothes.

COLD AND RAW THE NORTH WIND DOTH BLOW

Cold and raw the north wind doth blow,
Bleak in the morning early;
All the hills are covered with snow,
And winter's now come fairly.

AS TOMMY SNOOKS AND BETTY BROOKS

As Tommy Snooks and Bessy Brooks
Were walking out one Sunday,
Says Tommy Snooks to Bessy Brooks,
Tomorrow will be Monday.

COME, LET'S TO BED

Come, let's to bed,
Says Sleepy-head;
Tarry a while, says Slow;
Put on the pot,
Says Greedy-gut,
We'll sup before we go.

CROSS-PATCH

Cross-patch,
Draw the latch,
Sit by the fire and spin;
Take a cup,
And drink it up,
Then call your neighbours in.

CUCKOO, CUCKOO

Cuckoo, cuckoo, what do you do?
In April I open my bill;
In May I sing all day;
In June I change my tune;
In July away I fly;
In August away I must.

CUCKOO, CUCKOO, CHERRY TREE

Cuckoo, cuckoo, cherry tree,
Catch a bird, and give it me;
Let the tree be high or low,
Let it hail or rain or snow.

DAFFY-DOWN-DILLY

Daffy-down-dilly is new come to town,
With a yellow petticoat, and a green gown.

CURLY LOCKS

Curly locks, Curly locks,
Wilt thou be mine?
Thou shalt not wash dishes
Nor yet feed the swine;
But sit on a cushion
And sew a fine seam,
And feed upon strawberries,
Sugar and cream.

COME, BUTTER, COME

Come, butter, come,
Come, butter, come;
Peter stands at the gate
Waiting for a butter cake.
Come, butter, come.

IF ALL THE WORLD

I f all the world was paper,
And all the sea was ink,
If all the trees were bread and cheese,
What should we have to drink?

ICKLE OCKLE, BLUE BOCKLE

I ckle ockle, blue bockle,
Fishes in the sea,
If you want a pretty maid,
Please choose me.

IF

I f all the seas were one sea,
What a *great* sea that would be!
If all the trees were one tree,
What a *great* tree that would be!
And if all the axes were one axe,
What a *great* axe that would be!
And if all the men were one man,
What a *great* man that would be!
And if the *great* man took the *great* axe,
And cut down the *great* tree,
And let it fall into the *great* sea,
What a splish-splash that would be!

IF I HAD AS MUCH MONEY AS I COULD SPEND

I f I'D as much money as I could spend,
I never would cry old chairs to mend:
Old chairs to mend, old chairs to mend;
I never would cry old chairs to mend.

If I'd as much money as I could tell,
I never would cry old clothes to sell;

Old clothes to sell, old clothes to sell;
I never would cry old clothes to sell.

IN A COTTAGE IN FIFE

I n a cottage in Fife
Lived a man and his wife,
Who, believe me, were comical folk:
For, to people's surprise,
They both saw with their eyes,
And their tongues moved whenever they spoke.
When quite fast asleep,
I've been told that to keep
Their eyes open they could not contrive;
They walked on their feet,
And 'twas thought what they eat
Helped, with drinking, to keep them alive.

DINGTY, DIDDLETY

Dingty diddlety,
My mammy's maid,
She stole oranges,
I am afraid;
Some in her pocket,
Some in her sleeve,
She stole oranges,
I do believe.

SISSY!

DIDDLEY, DIDDLEY, DUMPTY

Diddley, diddley, dumpty,
The cat ran up the plum-tree,
Half a crown
To fetch her down,
Diddley, diddley, dumpty.

DING, DONG, BELL

Ding, dong, bell,
Pussy's in the well.
Who put her in?
Little Johnny Green.
Who pulled her out?
Little Tommy Stout.
What a naughty boy was that
To try to drown poor pussy cat,
Who never did him any harm,
And killed the mice in his father's barn.

DONKEY, DONKEY, OLD AND GREY

Donkey, donkey, old and grey,
Ope your mouth and gently bray;
Lift your ears and blow your horn,
To wake the world this sleepy morn.

DOCTOR FOSTER

Doctor Foster went to Gloucester
In a shower of rain;
He stepped in a puddle,
Right up to his middle,
And never went there again.

OOPS!

ORANGES AND LEMONS

Oranges and lemons,
Say the bells
of Saint Clement's.
You owe me five farthings,
Say the bells of Saint Martin's.
When will you pay me?
Say the bells of Old Bailey.
When I grow rich,
Say the bells of Shoreditch.
Pray when will that be?
Say the bells of Stepney.
I'm sure I don't know,
Says the great bell of Bow.
Here comes the candle
to light you to bed.
And here comes the chopper
to chop off your HEAD.

ONE, TWO, THREE, FOUR, FIVE

One, two, three, four, five,
Once I caught a fish alive,
Six, seven, eight, nine, ten,
Then I let it go again.
Why did you let it go?
Because it bit my finger so.
Which finger did it bite?
This little finger on the right.

ONE MISTY, MOISTY MORNING

One misty, moisty morning,
When cloudy was the weather,
I met a little old man
Clothed all in leather.

He began to compliment,
And I began to grin,
How do you do, and how do you do,
And how do you do again?

A, B, C

A, B, C, tumble down D,
The cat's in the cupboard
And can't see me.

GREAT A

Great A, little a,
Bouncing B,
The cat's in the cupboard
And can't see me.

GRANDFA' GRIG

Grandfa' Grig
Had a pig,
In a field of clover;
Piggy died,
Grandfa' cried,
And all the fun was over.

Here Is The Church

Here is the church,
Here is the steeple,
Open the doors
And here are the people.
Here's the parson going upstairs,
And here he is a-saying his prayers.

The Hart He Loves The High Wood

The hart he loves the high wood,
The hare she loves the hill;
The knight he loves his bright sword,
The lady loves her will.

Hector Protector

Hector Protector was dressed all in green;
Hector Protector was sent to the Queen.
The Queen did not like him,
No more did the King;
So Hector Protector was sent back again.

As Round As An Apple

As round as an apple,
As deep as a cup,
And all the king's horses
Cannot pull it up.

Four Stiff-Standers

Four stiff-standers,
Four dilly-danders,
Two lookers,
Two crookers,
And a wig-wag.

Flour Of England, Fruit Of Spain

Flour of England, fruit of Spain,
Met together in a shower of rain;
Put in a bag, tied round with a string;
If you tell me this riddle,
I'll give you a ring.

Old Mother Twitchett

Old Mother Twitchett has but one eye,
And a long tail which she can let fly,
And every time she goes over a gap,
She leaves a bit of her tail in a trap.

Black Within And Red Without

Black within and red without,
Four corners round about.

Little Billy Breek

Little Billy Breek
Sits by the reek,
He has more horns
Than all the king's sheep.

Two Brothers We Are

Two brothers we are,
Great burdens we bear,
On which we are bitterly pressed;
The truth is to say,
We are full all the day,
And empty when we go to rest.

In Marble Walls

In marble walls as white as milk
Lined with a skin as soft as silk,
Within a fountain crystal-clear,
A golden apple doth appear.
No doors there are to this stronghold,
Yet thieves break in and steal the gold.

THE THREE JOVIAL WELSHMEN

There were three jovial Welshmen,
As I have heard men say,
And they would go a-hunting
Upon St David's Day.

All the day they hunted
And nothing could they find,
But a ship a-sailing,
A-sailing with the wind.

One said it was a ship,
The other he said, Nay;
The third said it was a house,
With the chimney blown away.

And all the night they hunted
And nothing could they find,
But the moon a-gliding,
A-gliding with the wind.

One said it was the moon,
The other he said, Nay;
The third said it was a cheese,
And half of it cut away.

And all the day they hunted
And nothing could they find,
But a hedgehog in a bramble bush,
And that they left behind.

The first said it was a hedgehog,
The second he said, Nay;
The third said it was a pincushion,
And the pins stuck in wrong way.

And all the night they hunted
And nothing could they find,
But a hare in a turnip field,
And that they left behind.

The first said it was a hare,
The second he said, Nay;
The third said it was a calf,
And the cow had run away.

And all the day they hunted
And nothing could they find,
But an owl in a holly tree,
And that they left behind.

One said it was an owl,
The other he said, Nay;
The third said 'twas an old man,
And his beard growing grey.

THE THREE COOKS OF COLEBROOK

There were three cooks of Colebrook,
And they fell out with our cook;
And all was for a pudding he took
From the three cooks of Colebrook.

THE THREE SISTERS

There were three sisters in a hall,
There came a knight amongst them all;
Good morrow, aunt, to the one,
Good morrow, aunt, to the other,
Good morrow, gentlewoman, to the third,
If you were aunt,
As the other two be,
I would say good morrow,
Then, aunts, all three.

TWO BIRDS SAT ON A STONE

There were two birds sat on a stone,
One flew away, and then there was one,
The other flew after, and then there was none
And so the poor stone was left all alone,

SEE A PIN

See a pin and pick it up,
All the day you'll have good luck.
See a pin and let it lay,
Bad luck you'll have all the day.

SNAIL, SNAIL, PUT OUT YOUR HORNS

Snail, snail, put out your horns,
And I'll give you bread and barley corns.

SEE-SAW, MARGERY DAW

See-saw, Margery Daw,
Jacky shall have a new master;
Jacky shall have but a penny a day,
Because he can't work any faster.

RAIN, RAIN, GO AWAY

Rain, rain, go away,
Come again another day.

RAIN ON THE GREEN GRASS

Rain on the green grass,
And rain on the tree,
Rain on the house-top,
But not on me.

SHE SELLS SEA-SHELLS

She sells sea-shells on the sea shore;
The shells that she sells are sea-shells I'm sure.
So if she sells sea-shells on the sea shore,
I'm sure that the shells are sea-shore shells.

SEE-SAW, SACRADOWN

See-saw, Sacradown,
Which is the way
To London Town?
One foot up,
The other foot down,
That is the way
To London Town.

SING, SING

Sing, sing,
What shall I sing?
The cat's run away
With the pudding string!

Do, do,
What shall I do?
The cat's run away
With the pudding too!

JACK BE NIMBLE

J ack be nimble,
Jack be quick,
Jack jump over
The candlestick.

NAUTY PAUTY

N auty Pauty Jack-a-Dandy
Stole a piece of sugar candy
From the grocer's shoppy-shop,
And away did hoppy-hop.

THERE WAS AN OLD CROW

There was an old crow
  Sat upon a clod;
That's the end of my song,
  That's odd

THREE WISE MEN OF GOTHAM

Three wise men of Gotham
  Went to sea in a bowl
If the bowl had been stronger,
My story would have been longer.

TAFFY WAS A WELSHMAN

Taffy was a Welshman,
Taffy was a thief,
Taffy came to my house
And stole a piece of beef.

I went to Taffy's house,
Taffy wasn't in,
I jumped upon his Sunday hat
And poked it with a pin.

Taffy was a Welshman,
Taffy was a sham,
Taffy came to my house
And stole a leg of lamb.

I went to Taffy's house,
Taffy was not there,
I hung his coat and trousers
To roast before a fire.

Taffy was a Welshman,
Taffy was a cheat,
Taffy came to my house
And stole a piece of meat.

I went to Taffy's house,
Taffy wasn't home;
Taffy came to my house
And stole a marrow bone.

STAR LIGHT

Star light, star light,
First star I see tonight,
I wish I may, I wish I might,
Have the wish I wish tonight.

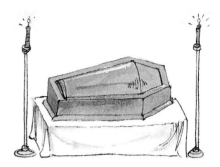

SOLOMON GRUNDY

Solomon Grundy,
Born on a Monday,
Christened on Tuesday,
Married on Wednesday,
Took ill on Thursday,
Worse on Friday,
Died on Saturday,
Buried on Sunday.
That is the end
Of Solomon Grundy.

SUKEY, YOU SHALL BE MY WIFE

Sukey, you shall be my wife
And I will tell you why;
I have got a little pig,
And you have got a sty;
I have got a dun cow,
And you can make good cheese;
Sukey, will you marry me?
Say Yes, if you please.

RAIN BEFORE SEVEN

Rain before seven,
Fine before eleven.

SHOE A LITTLE HORSE

Shoe a little horse,
Shoe a little mare,
But let the little colt
Go bare, bare, bare.

BARBER, BARBER

Barber, Barber, shave a pig,
How many hairs will make a wig?
"Four and twenty, that's enough."
Give the barber a pinch of snuff.

HERE AM I, LITTLE JUMPING JOAN

Here am I,
Little Jumping Joan;
When nobody's with me
I'm all alone.

HOT CROSS BUNS

Hot cross buns, hot cross buns;
One a penny poker,
Two a penny tongs,
Three a penny fire shovel,
Hot cross buns.

ANNA MARIA

Anna Maria she sat on the fire;
The fire was too hot, she sat on the pot;
The pot was too round, she sat on the ground;
The ground was too flat, she sat on the cat;
The cat ran away with Maria on her back.

AS I WALKED BY MYSELF

As I walked by myself
And talked to myself,
Myself said unto me,
Look to thyself,
Take care of thyself,
For nobody cares for thee.

I answered myself,
And said to myself
In the self-same repartee,
Look to thyself,
Or not to thyself,
The self-same thing will be.

150

CHRISTMAS COMES BUT ONCE A YEAR

Christmas comes but once a year,
And when it comes it brings good cheer,
A pocket full of money, and a cellar full of beer.

AS I WAS GOING TO BANBURY

As I was going to Banbury,
Upon a summer's day,
My dame had butter, eggs, and fruit,
And I had corn and hay;
Joe drove the ox, and Tom the swine,
Dick took the foal and mare,
I sold them all – then home to dine,
From famous Banbury fair.

CHRISTMAS IS COMING

Christmas is coming,
The geese are getting fat,
Please to put a penny
In the old man's hat.
If you haven't got a penny,
A ha'penny will do;
If you haven't got a ha'penny,
Then God bless you!

How To Play The Games

A-Hunting We Will Go

The children take partners, and form two lines. Holding hands, the first pair dance through the middle of the lines and back, then split and dance down the *outside* of the line. At the bottom, they pair up again and form an arch. Following the leaders, all the other children dance through the arch. Carry on until everyone has had a turn at making the arch.

The Big Ship Sails Through The Alley, Alley, O

The children form a line holding hands. At one end, a child puts his hand up against a wall or a tree to form an arch. The child at the other end dances round under the arch, followed by all the others. When the last child goes through, the one forming the arch is turned round, so that his other arm is crossing his body. The leader of the line dances round and goes through the space between the child touching the wall and his neighbour, turning the neighbour so that his arms are crossed.

This continues until all the children have been turned round and are standing with crossed arms. Now the leader reverses the actions, unwinding the line. When everyone is uncrossed, the children at the ends of the line join hands, and everyone skips in a ring.

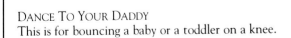

Here Is The Church

A finger game. For "Here is the church", clasp hands with fingers pointing down to palms, and knuckles pointing up. "Here is the steeple" – point first two fingers up in a steeple shape. "Open the doors" – turn hands over, so that palms are facing outward, with fingers crossing. "And here are the people" – wiggle your fingers!

"Here's the parson going upstairs" – cross hands so that palms face outward. Link the little finger of the right hand with the little finger of the left hand, and repeat until four fingers are linked. "And here he is saying his prayers" – with fingers still linked, turn hands round again so that the knuckles face your chest (this may need some practice if you've never done it). Rest one thumb on the clasped fingers. The other will stick up, and can be moved up and down to represent the praying parson.

Here We Go Round The Mulberry Bush

Dance in a ring for the first verse, then act out the words of each verse.

Dance To Your Daddy

This is for bouncing a baby or a toddler on a knee.

How Many Miles To Babylon?

One child is chosen to be "it", and "Babylon", or "home" is behind him. The other children stand in a row facing the single child. They ask the questions in the rhyme, and are answered by the child who's "it". On the last line, the children try and run past to reach Babylon or home safely. The single child tries to catch the runners. Anyone who is caught holds hands with the catcher and any other prisoners. As the rhyme is repeated, and the line of captured players becomes longer, it gets harder for the remaining players to run backwards and forwards.

I'M A LITTLE TEAPOT
Suit actions to words – for the second line, make a "handle" by putting one hand on a hip, and a "spout" by holding up the other arm, bent at elbow and wrist.

INCEY WINCEY SPIDER
A finger rhyme – use both hands. Fingers wriggle upwards for the spider, and downwards for the rain. For the sun, wave arms through the air in a gesture that suggests the sun shining on everything.

OH, DO YOU KNOW THE MUFFIN MAN?
Blindfold one child, then the others form a ring and walk round him, singing the first verse. At the end of the verse, the blindfolded child touches someone in the ring, who must then sing the second verse. If the blindfolded child can guess the identity of his prisoner, they change places. If not, the game goes on as before.

ONE, TWO, THREE, FOUR, FIVE
Count on fingers for the lines with numbers, and imitate the words with actions for the rest of the rhyme.

ORANGES AND LEMONS
Two children are chosen to form an arch. They decide who will be "oranges" and who will be "lemons". They hold their linked hands over their heads, and the other children pass underneath. When the line "Here comes a candle . . ." is reached, the children playing the arch bring their hands down to shoulder level, but raise them again, so that several children pass through until the word "head" is reached. The child who is trapped by the falling arms at this moment is secretly asked to choose whether to be an orange or lemon, and must join the side of his choice. When everyone has been caught, there is a tug-of-war between the two sides.

PAT-A-CAKE, PAT-A-CAKE, BAKER'S MAN
A clapping game. With a very small child simply clapping hands together would be fun. For a slightly older child, work out patterns – left hands clapped together, then right, then both hands together.

RIDE A COCK HORSE
This is for bouncing a baby on a knee.

RING-A-RING-O'-ROSES
Form a ring, and dance in a circle until the last line when everyone falls down!

ROUND AND ROUND THE GARDEN
Start by walking two fingers round the palm of a baby's hand. On the lines "One step, Two steps" walk your fingers up the baby's arm. At the line "Tickle him under there", tickle the baby under his arm.

SEE-SAW, SACRADOWN
This is for bouncing a baby on a knee.

THERE WAS A JOLLY MILLER
This needs equal numbers of boys and girls.

A "miller" is chosen – a boy – and stands in the centre of two rings: the inner one, girls; the outer one, boys.

The rings march or dance in opposite directions, and on the word "grab", every boy, including the miller, grabs a partner. Whichever boy fails to find a partner is the next miller.

THIS LITTLE PIGGY
A toe-counting rhyme for a baby. Start with the big toe. The "wee-wee-wee" for the little toe can turn into a tickling session!

TICKLY, TICKLY ON YOUR KNEE
A self-explanatory tickling game!

TO MARKET, TO MARKET, TO BUY A FAT PIG
Use to give a baby a knee ride.

TWO LITTLE DICKY BIRDS
A finger rhyme. Put both index fingers together for the first two lines, then raise the left one to show "Peter" and the right one to show "Paul". Make the birds fly away by hiding your fingers behind your back, then bring them back in order.

INDEX OF FIRST LINES

155

156